Class No. _J S-8_   Acc No. _C l 79503_

Author: _Anlberg, A_   Loc: _~~5 FEB 1999~~_

**LEABHARLANN
CHONDAE AN CHABHAIN**

~~1 1 AUG 1998~~

1. **This book may be kept three weeks. It is to be returned on / before the last date stamped below.**
2. **A fine of 20p will be charged for every week or part of week a book is overdue.**

2 1 JUL 1999

1 6 DEC 1999

-8 SEP 2000

2 1 MAR 2001

- 3 MAY 2001

2 2 APR 2002

Mr Cosmo
the Conjuror

by ALLAN AHLBERG

with pictures by
JOE WRIGHT

Puffin

Viking

PUFFIN/VIKING

Published by the Penguin Group
Penguin Books Ltd, 27 Wrights Lane, London W8 5TZ, England
Penguin Books USA Inc., 375 Hudson Street, New York, New York 10014, USA
Penguin Books Australia Ltd, Ringwood, Victoria, Australia
Penguin Books Canada Ltd, 10 Alcorn Avenue, Toronto, Ontario, Canada M4V 3B2
Penguin Books (NZ) Ltd, 182–190 Wairau Road, Auckland 10, New Zealand

Penguin Books Ltd, Registered Offices: Harmondsworth, Middlesex, England

First published 1980
10

Text copyright © Allan Ahlberg, 1981
Illustrations copyright © Joe Wright, 1981

Educational Advisory Editor: Brian Thompson

Printed and bound in Great Britain by
William Clowes Limited, Beccles and London
Set in Century Schoolbook by Filmtype Services Limited, Scarborough

ISBN Paperback 0 14 03.1237 4
ISBN Hardback 0–670–80575–0

It was early morning.
There was excitement in the town.
As if by magic, posters had appeared.
They said: MR COSMO IS COMING!

"Mr Cosmo is coming!"
everybody said.
"Mr Cosmo is coming!"
"Who is Mr Cosmo?"
On a hill outside the town,
a caravan appeared.

A horse was pulling it,
a performing dog was chasing it,
six pigeons were flying over it,
six rabbits were peeping out of it,
and *nobody* was driving it!

The caravan entered the town.
Everybody followed.
The caravan stopped.
Everybody gathered round.
The caravan door opened.
Everybody stared.
There in the doorway stood a man,
a woman, a boy and a girl.

"Good morning, ladies and gentlemen,"
said the man.
"Good morning, boys and girls!
I am Mr Cosmo the conjuror.
This is my wife;
these are my children."
"It's Mr Cosmo the conjuror!"
everybody said.
"That's his wife – those are his children!"

"Tonight there will be a big
open-air show!" Mrs Cosmo said.
"There's going to be a show!"
everybody said. "In the open air!"

"Everybody welcome!"
Miss Cosmo and Master Cosmo said.
"Everybody welcome!" everybody said.
"All of us!"
Now the caravan door closed.
Everybody went away.

The Cosmo family sat down
to breakfast.

"This seems like a nice little town,
my dear," Mrs Cosmo said.
"I agree," said Mr Cosmo.
"So do we," the children said.

After breakfast the children had
their conjuring lessons.

It tickles!

Mr Cosmo showed them
how to saw their mother in half.
Mrs Cosmo showed them how to
take eggs out of their father's ears.

In the afternoon Mr Cosmo did the shopping.
Mrs Cosmo made a cake.

The children went to the town school.
They surprised the teachers.
The performing dog played with the
town dogs.
He surprised them.

After tea the Cosmo family took a nap.
They needed a rest
before the big open-air show.

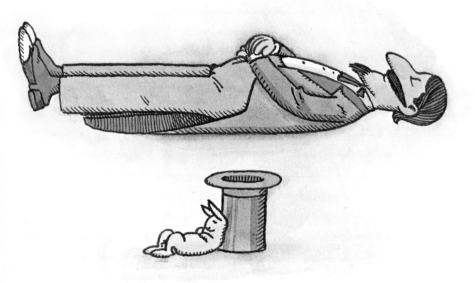

Now it was early evening.
As if by magic, lights had appeared.
They shone in the trees
beside the Cosmo caravan.
Everybody gathered round.
The big open-air show began.

"Ladies and gentlemen, boys and girls!"
Mr Cosmo said.
"For my first trick!"
Mr Cosmo pulled a rabbit
out of his hat.

Six rabbits!

"That's a rabbit!" everybody said.
He pulled five more rabbits out.
"That's five more!"
"Six altogether!"
"Six rabbits!" everybody said.
They all cheered.

The show went on.
Mr Cosmo did a trick with the pigeons.
"Look at those clever pigeons!"
everybody said.

Mrs Cosmo and the children
did a few tricks too.
The performing dog performed.
"Look at that clever dog!"
Everybody cheered louder than ever.

At last the show came to an end.
Miss Cosmo and Master Cosmo
collected money in their father's hat.
"Please put something in the hat,"
they said.

"I thought it was a hat for taking
things *out* of!" somebody said.

The Cosmo family waved good-bye.
Everybody cheered for the last time
– and went home to bed.

Mr Cosmo looked at his watch.
"It is time to leave," he said.
"I agree," said Mrs Cosmo.
"So do we," the children said.

It was late.
The lights in the trees were out.
The streets were quiet.
The moon shone bright in the black sky,
as the Cosmo caravan left the town.

The next morning there was excitement
in *another* town!
As if by magic, posters had appeared.
They said: MR COSMO IS COMING!

"Mr Cosmo is coming!" everybody said.
"Mr Cosmo is coming!"
"Who is Mr Cosmo?"

On a hill outside the town,
a caravan appeared.
A horse was pulling it,
a performing dog was chasing it,
six pigeons were flying over it,
six rabbits were peeping out of it,
and *nobody* was driving it!

The End